Great Groundhogs!

A HARRY & EMILY ADVENTURE

Karen Gray Ruelle

Holiday House / New York

To my favorite dad—

Beyond a shadow of a doubt the best dad ever!

Reading level: 2.6

Text and illustrations copyright © 2006 by Karen Gray Ruelle
All Rights Reserved
Printed in the United States of America
www.holidayhouse.com
First Edition
1 3 5 7 9 10 8 6 4 2

Library of Congress Cataloging-in-Publication Data
Ruelle, Karen Gray.
Great groundhogs! / Karen Gray Ruelle. —1st ed.
p. cm. — (A Harry & Emily adventure)
Summary: Tired of winter, Harry and his little sister Emily try to trap a groundhog
in their backyard and hope it will predict an early spring on Groundhog Day.
ISBN 0-8234-1930-4 (hardcover) — ISBN 0-8234-1964-9 (pbk.)
[1. Woodchuck—Fiction. 2. Groundhog Day—Fiction.] I. Title.
II. Series: Ruelle, Karen Gray. Harry & Emily adventure.
PZ7.R88525Gr 2005
[E]—dc22
2004060629

ISBN-13: 978-0-8234-1930-2
ISBN-10: 0-8234-1930-4

ISBN-13: 978-0-8234-1964-7 (pbk)
ISBN-10: 0-8234-1964-9 (pbk)

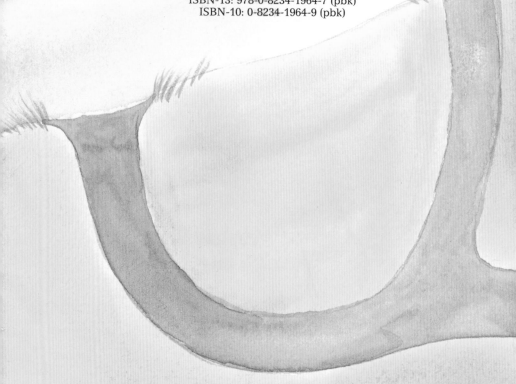

Contents

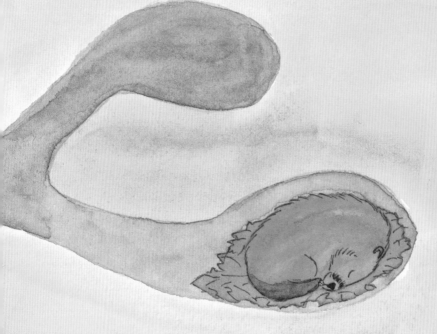

1. The Silliest Thing

"Tomorrow is Groundhog Day,"
  Harry told his little sister, Emily.
"Say *groundhog*
  when you wake up.
  Then you will have
  good luck all year."
"That's the silliest thing
  I've ever heard," said Emily.

"My teacher said groundhogs
tell us when spring is coming,"
said Harry.
"How do groundhogs
know about spring?"
Emily asked their parents.

"We have to watch them on
Groundhog Day," said their mother.
"If they have a shadow,
there will be six more
weeks of winter.
If they don't,
spring will come soon."
"That is even sillier
than saying *groundhog*
for good luck," said Emily.

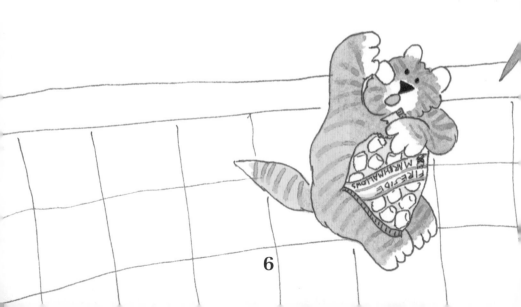

2. Do Groundhogs Oink?

Emily got her flashlight.
She looked under her bed.

She looked
in the closet.

She looked behind the pillow
on the living-room chair.
She even looked in the
cookie jar, just in case.
But she could not find
any groundhogs
or any groundhog shadows.

She said to Harry,
"I can't find
a groundhog anywhere."
"You won't find one in here,"
said Harry.
"Groundhogs live outdoors."
"Why didn't you tell me that?"
asked Emily.
"Why do you want to find
a groundhog?" asked Harry.

"I want to know
   when spring
   is coming,"
   said Emily.
"I am tired of the cold.
   I want to see flowers.
   I want to see new buds.
   I want it to be spring."

"Groundhog Day isn't
   until tomorrow," said Harry.
"If I find a groundhog today,
   I will know where to look
   for it tomorrow," said Emily.
"What do they look like anyway?
   Are they pink?
   Do they oink?"
"I don't think so," said Harry.
"Well, let's find out," said Emily.
   They looked in all of their books.
   They found pictures of bears
   and ducks and dragons.
   But no groundhogs.

They looked in the magazines
and the newspapers
in the recycling bin.
No groundhogs.
They searched on the computer.
At last they found a picture
of a groundhog.
It was not pink.

They found out that
groundhogs do not oink.
They have sharp teeth.
They squeal and bark and whistle.
Sometimes they are called
woodchucks or whistlepigs.
They found out that groundhogs
live in holes in the ground.
"I think we should look outside,"
said Emily.

3. Waiting for Groundhogs

"I don't see any groundhog holes,"
said Harry.

"I don't think we have any
groundhogs," said Emily.

"If we put out some good food,
maybe a groundhog will come,"
said Harry.

"We can dig a hole, too.
Then it will have
somewhere to live."
They dug a hole in the garden.
They dug a few extra holes,
in case the groundhog
had some friends.

"Now we have to put out some
groundhog food," said Emily.
"What do groundhogs eat?"
asked Harry.
"We can put out marshmallows,"
said Emily.
"We can put out grapes, too.
Everybody likes grapes.
And we can put out cookies,
for dessert."

Harry and Emily made a
yummy groundhog snack.
They put it next to
the groundhog holes.
Then they sat down to wait.

"What if the groundhog
gets thirsty?" asked Emily.
They went back into the house
to get a groundhog drink.
They put it out
with the groundhog snack.

Then Emily put some
pretty flowers in a flowerpot
to remind her of spring.
She put the flowerpot outside
where she could see it.

Harry and Emily waited
for a groundhog.
They waited all afternoon.
They waited until
the sun went down.
When it was too dark to see,
they went inside for dinner.

4. Any Shadows?

All night, Harry and Emily
kept waking up.
They looked out the window
to see if there were any groundhogs.

Finally they fell asleep.

Harry dreamed about shadows.

Emily dreamed about marshmallows
and sharp teeth.

At last it was morning.

"Groundhog shadows!" said Harry.

"Groundhog marshmallows!"
said Emily.

"We remembered to say *groundhog*!
This will be a lucky year!"

"I hope we are lucky enough
to see a groundhog," said Harry.

They went to tell their parents
Happy Groundhog Day.
Then they went outside.

"I see something!" said Emily.
Over by the groundhog holes,
there were birds and squirrels
and chipmunks.
But no groundhog.
"They're eating all
the groundhog food!"
said Harry.
"Now we'll never know about spring,"
said Emily.

"I don't see any groundhogs.
And I don't see any groundhog
shadows," said Harry.
"If there are no groundhog shadows,
spring is coming soon!" said Emily.
"I think you need a groundhog
for a groundhog shadow,"
said Harry.

"But there are no shadows today
   at all," said Emily.
"The birds and squirrels and
   chipmunks have no shadows.
   So if a groundhog were here,
   it would also have no shadow!"

"I think you are right," said Harry.
"But maybe we should call it
   Bird and Squirrel and Chipmunk Day
   instead of Groundhog Day."
"Whatever we call it,
   spring is on the way!" said Emily.

Just then they heard
a munching sound.
It was coming from the flowerpot.
Something was eating the flowers.

"Look!" said Harry. "A groundhog!"
And the groundhog
had no shadow at all.